The View at the Zoo

D0479860

ISBN: 978-0-8249-5669-1

WorthyKids
Hachette Book Group
1290 Avenue of the Americas
New York, NY 10104

Text copyright © 2015 by Kathleen Long Bostrom
Illustrations copyright © 2015 by Guy Francis
All rights reserved. No part of this publication may be reproduced or transmitted in any
form or by any means, electronic or mechanical, including photocopy, recording, or any
information storage and retrieval system, without permission in writing from the publisher.

WorthyKids is a registered trademark of Hachette Book Group, Inc.

Library of Congress Cataloging-in-Publication Data
Bostrom, Kathleen Long.
  A view at the zoo / by Kathleen Long Bostrom ; illustrated by Guy Francis.
    pages cm
  Originally published in 2011.
  Summary: Illustrations and rhyming text provide a glimpse of a day at the zoo as experienced
by the animals that live there.
  ISBN 978-0-8249-5669-1 (pbk. : alk. paper) [1. Stories in rhyme. 2. Zoo animals—Fiction.]
  I. Francis, Guy, illustrator. II. Title.
  PZ8.3.B64874Vie 2015
  [E]—dc23
                2014028412

Designed by Eve DeGrie
Printed and bound in China

APS
10 9 8 7

To my husband, Greg:
Life is a zoo, and I wouldn't have wanted
to share this life with any zookeeper but you.
Love always, always, always, Kathy

To my family, Lorien, Calvin, Sammy, Mattie, and Max,
who make our zoo a home. –G.F.

The View at the Zoo

Written by
Kathleen
Long Bostrom

Illustrated by
Guy Francis

WORTHY®
kids

Rise and shine! Attention, please!
Monkeys, get down from those trees!

Wake your cubs up, Mrs. Bear!
Mr. Lion, comb that hair!

All is ready.
Come on in!
Let the day of fun begin.

GIFT SHOP

My, what **silly things** they do, all these creatures at the zoo.

Walking on all kinds of feet,
dancing to an inner beat.

Babies riding on their backs,
on their bellies, snug in sacks.

Hear the silly sounds they speak,
as they howl and squawk
and shriek!

How they eat! They never stop!
That one looks about to pop!

See them prance and
primp and preen,
trying to stay neat and clean.

Some of them are quite a fright!
Watch your fingers—
they may bite!

Sun is setting in the sky. Everybody, say goodbye!
Please go home so we can sleep—
time for us to count our sheep.

Whew! They're leaving. Off they go!
They all put on quite a show!